Peppa Pig™

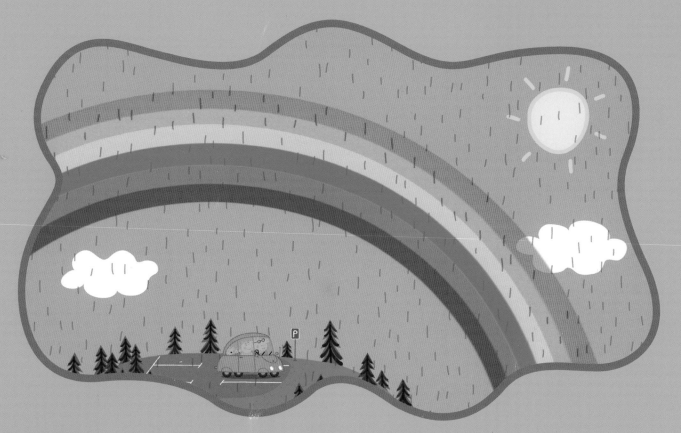

The Rainbow

Today, Peppa and her family are going for
a drive to the mountains.
"Are we nearly there yet?" asks Peppa.
"Hee! Hee! Not yet, Peppa," says Mummy Pig.

Peppa and George sigh.
Car trips can sometimes
be a bit boring!

"Let's play a game!" says Daddy Pig. "We each have to spot a car with our favourite colour." "Yippee!" say Peppa and George.

Candy Cat and her mummy are driving in their car.
"Green is my favourite colour. I win!" Daddy Pig says.
Candy and Peppa wave at each other.

Look! Danny Dog is driving in
Grandad Dog's orange truck.
"It's orange! So I win!" says Mummy Pig.
"This is a silly game! There isn't a red car
anywhere!" says Peppa.

"There is *one* red car on the road," says
Daddy Pig. "What colour is our car?"
"It's red!" says Peppa. "My favourite colour!
I win! Yay!"

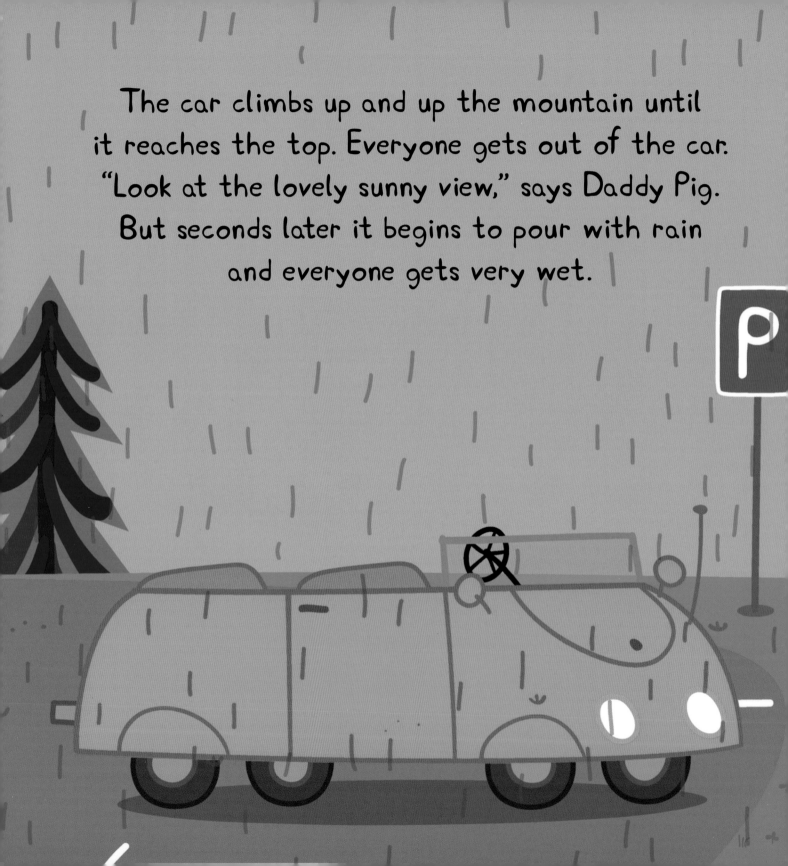

The car climbs up and up the mountain until
it reaches the top. Everyone gets out of the car.
"Look at the lovely sunny view," says Daddy Pig.
But seconds later it begins to pour with rain
and everyone gets very wet.

Daddy Pig spots Miss Rabbit's
ice cream stall.
"Four ice creams, please,
Miss Rabbit," says Daddy Pig.
"What flavours would you
like?" asks Miss Rabbit.
"Mint, orange, strawberry
and blueberry, please,"
says Daddy Pig.

Everyone is very happy. They all have ice cream in their favourite colour! They sit in the car, eating their yummy ice cream and watching the rain fall. "Mmmm, yummy!" Peppa says.

"Look! The sun has come out!" says Mummy Pig. "A rainbow! Hee! Hee!" giggles Peppa. Peppa and George love rainbows. "It has all our favourite colours in it," says Mummy Pig.

"What's at the end of the rainbow?" asks Peppa.
"Treasure!" says Mummy Pig.
"Can we go and find it?" says Peppa.
"That sounds like fun! Let's go," says Daddy Pig.

"Where's our rainbow gone?" asks Peppa.
"It's moved to the next hill!" says Mummy Pig.
"Oh, you cheeky rainbow!" giggles Peppa.
"Quick! Let's catch it!" says Daddy Pig,
starting the car again.

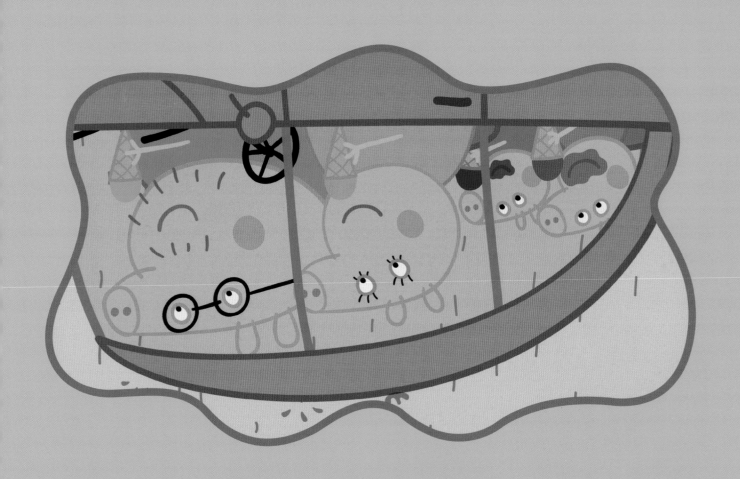

Splash!

"Yes, I have!" says Daddy Pig with a smile.
"It's a big muddy puddle!"
They all jump in the puddle together.
"This is the best rainbow treasure
ever!" says Peppa.

Splish!

"Don't worry, George. Maybe the rainbow has left some treasure behind," says Mummy Pig.

Daddy Pig spots something. "Have you found the rainbow's treasure, Daddy?" asks Peppa.

They drive in the car to the next hill.
"It's stopped raining," says Daddy Pig.
"And the rainbow has gone!" says Peppa
as the family jump out of the car.
"Waaa!" cries George.